AYMAN

בס"ד

This book belongs to:

לה׳ הארץ ומלואה

Yoel Margolis

Hachai

Please read it to me!

The Bravest Fireman

Dedicated to
New York City Firefighters –
You are all the bravest.

The Bravest Fireman

To my dedicated "accountant," who has always tallied up my credits and disregarded my debits. L.Z.

To my mother, for the gift of "eresokol," with love. L.M.D.

First Edition – Nissan 5758 / April 1998
Second Impression – Shevat 5762 / January 2002

ISBN: 0-922613-88-5
LCCN: 97-77998

HACHAI PUBLISHING
Brooklyn, New York 11218
Tel: 718-633-0100 Fax: 718-633-0103
www.hachai.com   info@hachai.com
Printed in China

Glossary

Hashem – G-d   **Tehillim** – Psalms
Torah – Jewish Scripture and Oral Tradition; Five Books of Moses

the Bravest Fireman

by Leah Zytman
illustrated by Leah Malka Diskind

Hachai
PUBLISHING

Once there was a
fire on my block.

The firemen came to our house at night and told us to get out of bed and wait outside.

It was a windy night, and they didn't want sparks from the fire to catch on to our house.

We waited in a safe place with our neighbors and watched the flames.

"Please, don't let anyone get hurt," I whispered to Hashem.

When I grow up, I'm going to be a fireman.

I will be the strongest and bravest fireman in my company.

As soon as the alarm goes off,
I will slide down the pole.

The firemen will race to our truck, and I will drive – faster and faster – not a second to waste!

While the other firefighters connect the hose to the fire hydrant, I'll go inside to rescue the people.

The burning building is
    hot and full of smoke.
But someone must go in.

I will be the one.

I will say my Tehillim,
and I won't be afraid.

The smoke will sting my eyes and fill my throat. But the Torah says, "Saving one life is like saving the world."

I won't let the smoke stop me.

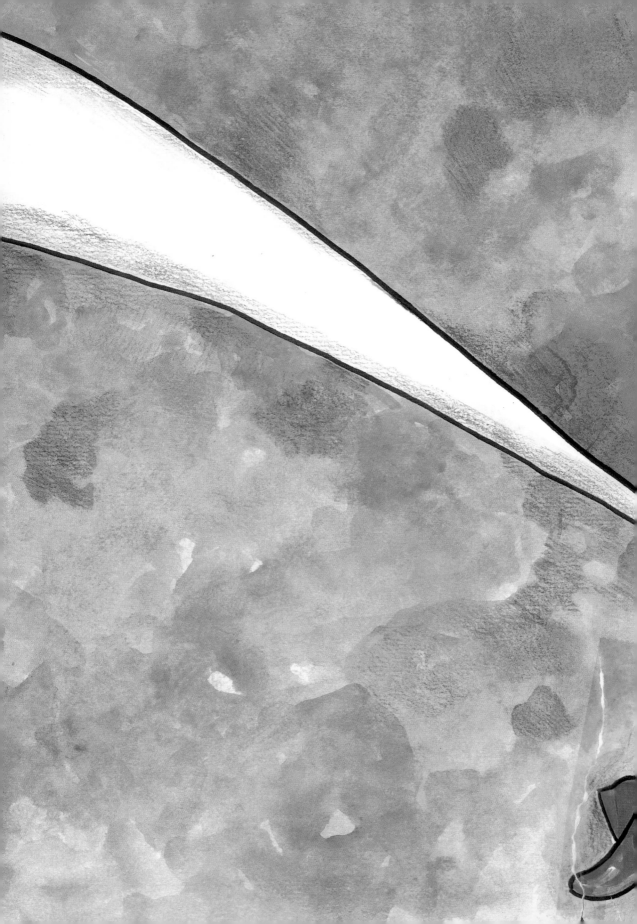

When all the people are safely out, I'll help the other firemen spray water on the flames.

"Ari," the Fire Chief will say, "you've done enough. You may rest if you want to."

But I won't.

I will go back inside
the building to make
sure every bit of the
fire is out.

When no smoke or
burning embers are
left, I will know the job
is done.

The firemen and I will shake each other's hands. We have worked hard and been a good team.

I will say, "You guys are great!"

The firemen will lift me high on their shoulders and sing, "Three cheers for Ari, the bravest and strongest fireman!"